The Amazing Adventures of

Wonderpig

The worlds first and only Vegan Superhero

Saving the animals, the environment and
the human race from suffering and destruction
in a nice Vegan way.

Written and Illustrated
by

Phil Tutton

Vegan love
Wonderpig

The Amazing Adventures of WonderpiG
Volume One

This book is dedicated to;
Tim, Noah and Jack for giving me the chance,
To Fran for listening,
To Marc and Hayley for inspiration,
To Puressence for keeping me sane,
To Mum and Dad for having me but most of all,
To Amina without whom none of this would have ever happened.

Published by:
Wonderpig Publishing
62 Jalland Street
Hull
HU8 8RB
Printed in the UK by Fisk Printers Ltd, Hull, HU9 1SD on Recycled Paper

WONDERPIG
THE VEGAN SUPERHERO......
WILLIAM WAS A HAPPY PIG IN MUCK
ALL THE OTHER ANIMALS LOVED HIM.
BUT THE MILD MANNERED PORCINE HID A SECRET, IF A WRONG NEEDS RIGHTING HE BECOMES.....
WONDERPIG
THE WORLDS ONLY VEGAN SUPERHERO!

OH MY GOD!
WHATS UP COCK?
ONE SUNNY DAY.........
I'VE JUST SEEN WHERE EGGS COME FROM.... ITS AWFUL.
HHMMMM...
FOOD EDUCATION SEEMED TO BE SOMEWHAT LACKING.......
THIS WAS A JOB FOR...
WP
EGG SHED
THE VEGAN SUPERHERO DECIDED TO INVESTIGATE.
WHEN HIS SUPER SENSES ADJUSTED TO THE STENCH, NOISE AND GLOOM, HE WAS HORRIFIED...
HUNDREDS OF CAGES, 1000's OF HENS!

THE CAGED BIRDS TOLD WONDERPIG THAT LIVING IN THESE HIDEOUS CONDITIONS WAS 'NORMAL' FOR MILLIONS OF EGG LAYING CHICKENS IN BRITAIN.

ALTHOUGH THE ENORMOUS SHED WAS FULL OF POO WONDERPIG WAS NOT HAPPY! IN FACT HE WAS STARTING TO GET VERY CROSS. ANIMAL ABUSE UPSET HIM AND THIS WAS SERIOUS ABUSE, SO HE DECIDED TO DO SOMETHING ABOUT IT.....

HE WAS NOW IN A 'FOWL' MOOD AND WENT LOOKING FOR THE FARMER.

WONDERPIG DIDNT BOTHER KNOCKING. HE FOUND THE FARMERS FAMILY AND TRUE TO HIS VEGAN VALUES USED GENTLE PERSUASION AND BLACKMAIL ABOUT THE FARMERS WEEKEND HOBBIES TO MAKE THEM SEE SENSE.

USING HIS SUPERHERO POWERS HE MADE A SMALL CAGE, FILLED IT WITH THE FAMILY AND TOLD THEM TO GET ON WITH THEIR JOBS!......

IT WASNT LONG BEFORE THEY REALISED WHERE THEY HAD BEEN GOING WRONG.

WONDERPIG FELT A BIT BETTER.

WITH THE HELP OF MANY ANIMAL LOVING FRIENDS, WONDERPIG RESCUSED THE BIRDS AND DESTROYED THEIR PRISONS. THE SICK BIRDS WERE TREATED IN HOSPITAL AND THE HEALTHY ONES FINISHED THEIR LIVES IN PEACE AND FREEDOM AS NATURE INTENDED.

THIS WAS A GOOD DAYS WORK BUT WAS ONLY THE START AND WONDERPIG KNEW THERE WAS MUCH MORE TO DO........

WONDERPIG CELEBRATED HIS SUCCESS WITH HIS BEST FRIENDS AND A BUCKET OF VEGAN WINE.

HE TOOK A DAY OFF AND RELAXED AS ONLY A PIG COULD, WAITING FOR THE NEXT CALL FOR HIS HELP.......

WONDERPIG
THE VEGAN SUPERHERO

WILLIAM WAS ENJOYING A BUCKET OF VEGAN SWILL……

SURROUNDED BY HIS FRIENDS

ALTHOUGH HE WAS A LAID BACK FRIENDLY PIGGY, WHEN HE DISCOVERS ANY ANIMAL ABUSE HE BECOMES SLIGHTLY CROSS AND

WONDERPIG

ONE SUNNY DAY HE CAME ACROSS A GLUM LOOKING TWO DAY OLD CALF...

THE TEARFUL CALF EXPLAINED THAT ALTHOUGH HE WAS ONLY 2 DAYS OLD HE WAS BEING TAKEN AWAY FROM HIS MUM!

WILLIAM WAS SUPRISED BY THIS

AND WENT OFF TO INVESTIGATE.....

HE FOUND THE CALFS MOTHER AND ASKED HER ABOUT HER SONS CLAIMS

THE POOR COW EXPLAINED THAT HER CHILDREN WERE TAKEN AWAY FROM HER AFTER 2 DAYS, THEN SHE WAS MADE PREGNANT AGAIN AND AGAIN AND..... THIS WAS A JOB FOR....

WONDERPIG WATCHED AS HUNDREDS OF TINY CALVES WERE LOADED INTO BIG, HOT LORRIES...

HE WAS RATHER UPSET BY THIS AND DECIDED TO DO SOMETHING ABOUT IT.

WONDERPIG SET OFF TO LOOK FOR THE FARMER RESPONSIBLE.

THE SUPERHERO FOUND THE SMALL FARMHOUSE AND THE FARMER.....

THE SLIGHTLY SCARED FARMER TRIED TO EXPLAIN WHY THE CALVES HAD TO BE TAKEN FROM THEIR MOTHERS AFTER JUST A DAY OR TWO.

WONDERPIG LISTENED TO THE FARMER, DECIDED IT WAS ALL "BULLOCKS" AND FORMULATED A PLAN TO SHOW THE FARMER THE ERROR OF HIS WAYS. HE TOOK THE FARMERS YOUNG CHILDREN WITH HIM AND PUT THEM INTO A SMALL DARK TRAILER.....

WONDERPIG DROVE THE TRAILER AROUND THE COUNTRYSIDE WITH HIS DUAL FUELED ECO CAR.

IT WAS A HOT DAY AND WITH NO WATER THE CHILDREN WERE NOT ENJOYING IT.

WONDERPIG RAPIDLY MADE SOME SMALL WOODEN CRATES.

WONDERPIG WAS ABOUT TO FILL THE CRATES.

WHEN THE FARMER ASKED HIM TO STOP WONDERPIG COMPLAINED AS HE COULDN'T SEND THEM TO BELGIUM TO BE FORCE FED GROWTH HORMONES AND ANTIBIOTICS BEFORE SENDING THEM TO AN ABBATOIR.....

AT LAST THE FARMER ADMITTED HE WAS WRONG.

THE FARMER AGREED TO STOP DAIRY FARMING AND LET HIS COWS LIVE IN PEACE.

HE STOPPED BREEDING AND MILKING HIS COWS AND STARTED GROWING SOYA BEANS AND CARROTTS. THE MILKING PARLOUR WAS CONVERTED TO A RECORDING STUDIO.

WONDERPIG WAS VERY HAPPY TO HAVE SAVED ALL THOSE COWS AND CALVES FROM A FATE OF DEATH!......

THE FREE COWS PARTIED ALL NIGHT

HIS WORK FINISHED. WONDERPIG RETURNED TO HIS FARM AND TO NORMALITY...... 'TIL NEXT TIME.

WONDERPIG

THE VEGAN SUPERHERO

WILLIAM THE PIG WAS CHILLING OUT IN HULL LISTENING TO PURESSENCE ON HIS MP3 PLAYER. HE WAS A HAPPY VEGAN PIG..

WILLIAM LIVED IN AN ANIMAL SANCTUARY WITH LOTS OF HAPPY, RESCUED FRIENDS. ALL WAS PEACEFUL...

IT WAS A LUXURIOUS PLACE FOR THE ANIMALS TO FEEL SAFE FROM EVIL HUMAN ABUSE.. THEY WERE ALL BEST MATES AND HAD EVERYTHING THEY COULD WANT!

WILLIAM WAS ENJOYING A BUCKET OF VEGAN SWILL WHEN A SMALL PUPPY RAN UP TO HIM, CRYING.
HE LISTENED TO THE SMALL PUPPY'S TAIL OF WOE
WILLIAM HEARD HOW THE PUP WAS BRED ON A PUPPY FARM WHERE THEY TRIED TO REMOVE HIS TAIL THEN PUT HIM UP FOR SALE IN A PET SHOP WINDOW.
SHOCKED HE DECIDED THIS WAS A JOB FOR ....
WP
HIS SUPERSENSES TOLD HIM THIS WAS IT.
WONDERPIG SET OFF TO FIND THE PUPPY FARM...
HE QUICKLY SPOTTED A NASTY LOOKING, BROKEN SHED

INSIDE THE LEAKY SHED THERE WERE CAGES OF DOGS WAITING TO PRODUCE PUPPIES.....
WONDERPIG WAS LIVID AND PLOTTED HIS REVENGE AGAINST THE OFFENDERS
WITH THE HELP OF SOME LOYAL SUPPORTERS THEY LIBERATED THE DOGS BEFORE REHOMING THEM...
THEY THEN DISMANTLED AND RECYCLED THE SHED.......
HAVING WRECKED THEIR BUSINESS WONDERPIG WENT LOOKING FOR THE PUPPY FARM OWNERS.........
WP

WONDERPIG REMOVED THE CHILDREN FROM THE HOUSE ONE BY ONE.

HE RENTED A PET SHOP AND PUT THE CHILDREN UP FOR SALE

WONDERPIG TOOK THE YOUNGEST BOY AND TREATED HIM LIKE A PUPPY.

THE DOG BREEDER REALISED THAT IT WAS WRONG TO BREED AND SELL ANIMALS FOR PROFIT WHEN SO MANY HOMELESS DOGS NEED HELP........

WONDERPIG FOUND ALL THE PROFITS THEY HAD MADE FROM SELLING PUPPIES...

HE MADE THE OFFENDERS GIVE ALL THEIR EXCESS CASH TO THE LOCAL DOG SHELTER.....

WONDERPIG WAS CHEERING UP....

THE OFFENDERS TURNED THE PUPPY FARM INTO A PLAYGROUND.

THE HOMELESS DOGS LIVED IN LUXURY

WILLIAM CELEBRATED WITH A BUCKET OF VEGAN BEER BACK ON THE FARM.

WONDERPIG
IS IT A BIRD? IS IT A PLANE? NO ITS......WONDERPIG!
WILLIAM WAS PLAYING WITH HIS PAL HAYLEY ON THE FARM IN HULL, ONE HOT SUNNY DAY.
HE WAS A BIT WORRIED ABOUT GLOBAL WARMING AS IT WAS MID JANUARY.
SPF 80
FOOD STORE
BEA
BECAUSE OF THE LARGE NUMBER OF RESCUED ANIMALS AT THE SANCTUARY, MONEY WAS TIGHT AND THE FOOD WAS GETTING LOW
"RUMBLE"
BEING A NATURAL PIG WILLIAM GOT HUNGRY QUICKLY BUT THE GOATS MANAGED BY EATING ANYTHING! HE MADE A DECISION TO DO SOMETHING ABOUT BOTH PROBLEMS......

FIRST HE DECIDED THIS WAS A JOB FOR.....

WONDERPIG!

HAVING NO REAL FINGERS TYPING WAS DIFFICULT FOR WONDERPIG SO HE GOT HAYLEYS BROTHER, MARC, TO TYPE TWO LETTERS ON HIS COMPUTER WHICH HE THEN PRINTED AND POSTED.
HE WAITED TO SEE IF THERE WAS ANY RESPONSE......

THE FIRST REPLY WAS A GOOD SPONSORSHIP DEAL WITH YAOH PRODUCTS MEANING THE ANIMALS ALL COULD EAT.

NEXT DAY THE OTHER LETTER BEGAN TO HAVE AN EFFECT

THEN OUR HERO GOT A CALL FROM A T.V. COMPANY REQUESTING AN INTERVIEW TO EXPLAIN HIS THEORY.

WONDERPIG REFUSED THE OFFER OF A POLLUTING LIMO TO THE TV STUDIO AND TOOK HIS OWN ENVIRONMENTALLY COOL WAY

ALTHOUGH HE WAS ALREADY REALLY GOOD LOOKING HE NEEDED A BIT OF MAKE UP BEFORE HIS TV DEBUT

BEING THE CARING VEGAN SUPERHERO HE INSISTED ON THE MAKE UP BEING CRUELTY FREE AND VEGAN. HE ALSO USED HIS OWN YAOH VEGAN MOISTURISER.

WONDERPIG WAS LOOKING FORWARD TO EDUCATING THE WORLD ON HOW TO SAVE THE PLANET VEGAN STYLE.......

THIS WAS HIS BIG CHANCE TO MAKE A DIFFERENCE TO THE WORLD.

WONDERPIG WAS TAKING THIS VERY SERIOUSLY ....

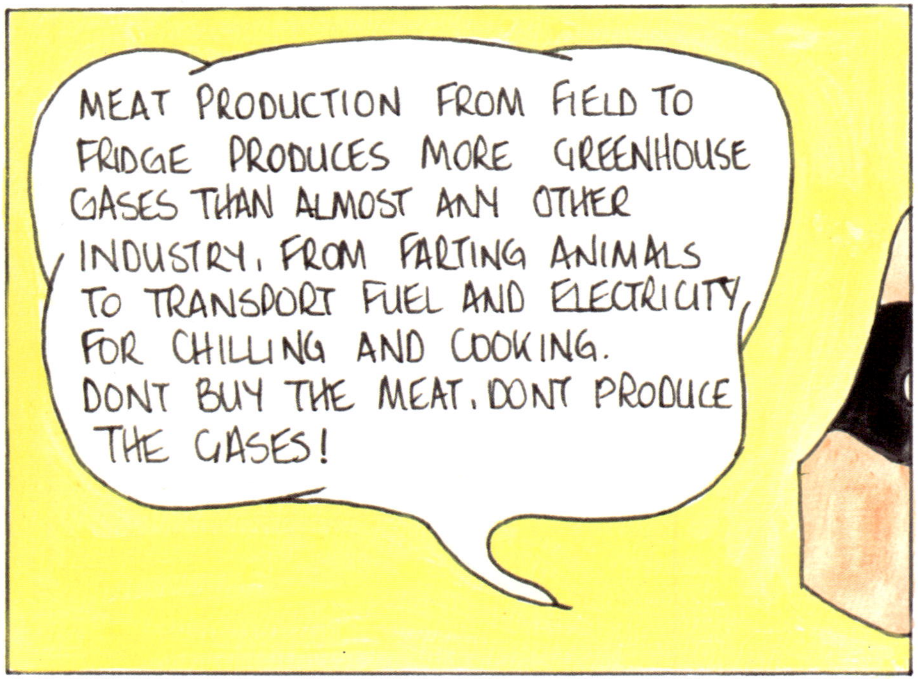

OUR HERO STARTED TOUGH AND GOT TOUGHER!

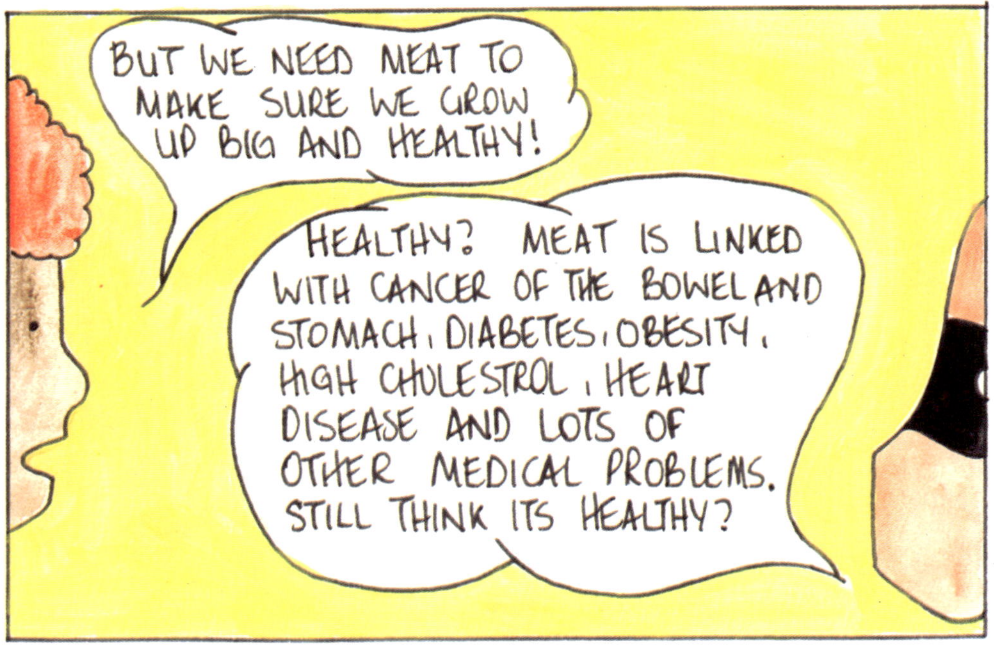

WHAT ABOUT BUILDING STRONG BONES & MUSCLES?
GORILLAS ARE YOUR NEAREST GENETIC RELATIVES THEY ARE VEGANS! ARE THEY WEAK & PUNY?
BUT BY INCREASING TAXES THAT WILL SORT OUT THE ENVIRONMENT SURELY?
IF YOU ARE STUPID ENOUGH TO BUY AN OVERPRICED, 4x4, URBAN RHINO DODGER, THEN YOU WONT MIND PAYING EXTRA TAXES. AND ONE HUMAN GOING VEGAN IS BETTER THAN REMOVING ONE GAS GUZZLER FROM THE ROADS.
I SEE YOUR POINT!
WE NEED ACTION NOT TAXES. MAKE IT LAW THAT ALL NEW HOUSES FIT SOLAR PANELS. LOWER COSTS, LOTS OF JOBS, ENERGY USE SLASHED. SIMPLE!
BUT DO YOU GET A GOOD BALANCED DIET AND WHERE DO YOUR SUPERPOWERS COME FROM?
A TOTALLY PLANT BASED DIET CAN BE THE BEST DIET FOR EVERYONE. THE ONLY PEOPLE WHO WANT YOU TO EAT MEAT, FISH AND DAIRY PRODUCTS ARE THE PEOPLE MAKING MONEY OUT OF YOU. MY SUPERPOWERS COME FROM YAOH HEMP BARS. TASTY, NUTRIOUS ENERGY PACKED VEGAN SNACKS!

AREN'T YOU DEPRIVING YOURSELF FOR NO REASON?
I ONLY DEPRIVE MYSELF OF DISEASE AND ILLNESS. MY DIET MEANS I AM HEALTHIER, THE PLANET IS HEALTHIER AND NO ANIMALS SUFFER
WELL I MUST ADMIT I'M CONVERTED. THESE YAOH SNACKS ARE YUMMY.
YAOH
THE TV SHOW WAS SEEN AROUND THE WORLD AND OVERNIGHT THE PLANET WENT VEGAN WITH GREAT EFFECT ON THE ENVIRONMENT
BACK IN HULL JANUARY RETURNED TO NORMAL AS THE PLANET HEALED
WILLIAM, MARC AND HAYLEY CELEBRATED IN THE SNOW. THEY PUT AWAY THEIR YAOH SUNCREAM TIL NEXT SUMMER.

WONDERPIG

ONE PIG CAN MAKE A DIFFERENCE

WILLIAM WAS RELAXING AT HOME ON THE FARM IN HULL.

HE HAD A NICE PAD WHERE HE ENJOYED VARIOUS HOBBIES.

LIFE ON THE FARM WASNT ALL PLAY. JOBS HAD TO BE DONE!

ALL THE HARD WORK GAVE WILLIAM A GOOD APPETITE.

HE ENTERTAINED ALL HIS FREINDS FOR HOURS ON END.

ONE DAY A YOUNG COW CAME TO THE FARM IN A DISTRESSED STATE....

WILLIAM LISTENED TO HER TALE OF WOE...

THE COW EXPLAINED THAT ALTHOUGH SHE WAS ONLY FIVE YEARS OLD SHE HAD ALREADY HAD FIVE CALVES AND WAS EXPECTING AGAIN BEFORE BEING SLAUGHTERED BY THE TIME SHE WAS ONLY SEVEN. THE POOR COW WAS PHYSICALLY AND MENTALLY KNACKERED. SHE THEN TOLD WILLIAM A FOUL SECRET.........

A SHOCKED WILLIAM DECIDED THIS WAS A JOB FOR......

HE SET OFF IN SEARCH OF SOME ANSWERS.....

HIS SEARCH TOOK LONGER THAN EXPECTED BUT.....
SECRET DOCUMENT STORAGE FACILITY
EVENTUALLY HE FOUND WHAT HE WAS LOOKING FOR.....
HE DIDNT BOTHER WITH THE FRONT DOOR.
MILITARY SECRETS →
SPORT SECRETS →
DAIRY SECRETS ←
CONSPIRACY THEORIES ↑
RELIGIOUS SECRETS ←
UFO/ALIEN SECRETS →
HE HAD SOME HELP FINDING WHAT HE WANTED....
W.C.
WONDERPIG QUICKLY GOT TO THE ROOM HE WANTED..
C-D
F-G
D-E
G-H
HE WAS SUPRISED AT JUST HOW MANY SECRETS WERE BEING KEPT FROM US.....

A-B
WONDERPIG PERSUADED SECURITY TO LET HIM FIND WHAT HE WANTED.
USING METHODICAL SEARCH PROCEDURES WONDERPIG BEGAN THE PAPER HUNT.
GOT IT!
EVENTUALLY HE FOUND WHAT HE WAS LOOKING FOR.
BARF!
YEUGH!
A-B
THE TRUTH WAS A LITTLE HARD TO STOMACH.....
WONDERPIG DISCOVERED THAT SOME COWS SUFFER FROM AN INFECTION CALLED MASTITIS WHICH CAN GET INTO THE MILK. THE GOVERNMENT ALLOWS 400.000.000 MASTITIS PUS CELLS IN EACH LITRE OF MILK DRANK BY HUMANS!!!
THATS A WHOLE ZIT IN EVERY GLASS!

WONDERPIG MAILED THE EVIDENCE TO THE PRESS.

EVEN TOUGH JOURNALISTS WERE SHOCKED BY THE TRUTH....

WHILE OTHERS JUST HAD NO IDEA.

THE JOURNALIST ASKED SOME IN DEPTH QUESTIONS WHICH WONDERPIG ANSWERED WITH STYLE.

JOURNALIST: BUT SURELY MILK IS A NATURAL, HEALTHY FOOD!
WONDERPIG: IF ITS NATURAL WHY ARE YOU THE ONLY SPECIES ON THE PLANET TO DRINK MILK AS ADULTS?
JOURNALIST: BUT YOU NEED IT TO GROW STRONG BONES AND MUSCLES.
WONDERPIG: GORILLAS ARE CLOSE GENETIC RELATIVES TO YOU, THEY DONT DRINK MILK, ARE THEY WEAK AND PUNY?
JOURNALIST: BUT SURELY MILK IS GOOD FOR YOU.....

WONDERPIG: NO NO NO. ITS FULL OF GROWTH HORMONES WHICH ARE LINKED TO BREAST CANCER. IT CAN LEAD TO OBESITY AND BOWEL DISORDERS. ITS LINKED TO ASTHMA, ECZEMA AND MANY OTHER MEDICAL PROBLEMS AND THE COWS SUFFER BEFORE BEING KILLED VERY YOUNG.

DAILY NEWS
MILKY HORROR SECRET
"GROSS"
"YUK"
"COWS RELIEVED"
SHOCK!
GOD IS A WOMAN
SIDENT GOES VEGAN
THE FOLLOWING DAY THE NEWS HIT THE STREETS AND SPREAD AROUND THE WORLD RAPIDLY....
SEE! WE WERE RIGHT ALL THIS TIME.....
OH CRAP!
NO ONE ANYWHERE EVER BOUGHT ANY DAIRY PRODUCTS AGAIN.
WP
2
SOME COWS FOUND OTHER WAYS TO ENTERTAIN THEMSELVES.
OTHERS GOT WORK AS LAWNMOWERS ON GOLF COURSES....
THE FARMERS GREW VEGETABLES AND BEANS TO MAKE US EVEN MORE HEALTHY.

WONDERPIG WAS OVER THE MOON WITH HIS STUNNING VICTORY.
BUT HE WANTED TO FIND A WAY TO CELEBRATE IN A STYLE FITTING SUCH A DRAMATIC CHANGE IN THE WORLDS HEALTH.
WP
MUSIC WEB
AFTER A QUICK SEARCH ON THE INTERNET AND 20 MINUTES ON THE TELEPHONE, THE CELEBRATION WAS SORTED....
WP
JAMES AND THE REST OF PURESSENCE PUT ON A FREE SHOW FOR ALL THE VEGANS WHO ROCKED FOR HOURS!
THE WORLDS POPULATION GOT HEALTHIER AND LIGHTER AND WILLIAM WENT BACK TO "NORMAL" LIFE ON THE FARM.

I hope you enjoyed reading The Amazing Adventure of WonderpiG.
For more information on the issues in the book here are some addresses;

www.myspace.com/philtutton

www.yaoh.co.uk

www.peta.org.uk www.myspace.com/peta2

The Vegan Society, Donald Watson House, 7 Battle Rd, St Leonards on Sea,
East Sussex. TN37 7AA
www.vegansociety.com

Viva, 8 York Court, Wilder Street, Bristol. BS2 8QH
www.viva.org.uk

Animal Aid, The Old Chapel, Bradford, Tonbridge, Kent. TN9 1AW
www.animalaid.org.uk

Look after your planet, it's the only one you'll get.